THE MAGIC PURSE

OTHER BOOKS BY YOSHIKO UCHIDA

Journey Home *illustrated by Charles Robinson*
A Jar of Dreams
The Best Bad Thing
The Happiest Ending
The Two Foolish Cats *illustrated by Margot Zemach*

WRITTEN AND ILLUSTRATED BY KEIKO NARAHASHI

I Have a Friend

OTHER BOOKS ILLUSTRATED BY KEIKO NARAHASHI

Who Said Red? *by Mary Serfozo*
Who Wants One? *by Mary Serfozo*
Rain Talk *by Mary Serfozo*
The Little Band *by James Sage*
My Grandfather's Hat *by Melanie Scheller*

(MARGARET K. McELDERRY BOOKS)

Text copyright © 1993 estate of Yoshiko Uchida
Illustrations copyright © 1993 by Keiko Narahashi

Margaret K. McElderry Books
Macmillan Publishing Company
866 Third Avenue
New York, NY 10022
Macmillan Publishing Company is part of the Maxwell Communication Group of Companies.
First edition   Printed in Hong Kong by South China Printing Company (1988) Ltd.   10   9   8   7   6   5   4   3   2   1   The text of this book is set in Cartier. The illustrations are rendered in watercolors.

Maxwell Macmillan Canada, Inc.
1200 Eglinton Avenue East
Suite 200
Don Mills, Ontario M3C 3N1

Library of Congress Cataloging-in-Publication Data
Uchida, Yoshiko.
   The magic purse / Yoshiko Uchida ; illustrated by Keiko Narahashi. — 1st ed.   p.   cm.
   Summary: After facing danger and demons to help a young woman, a poor farmer receives a magic purse that always refills itself with gold.
   ISBN 0-689-50559-0
   [1. Fairy tales. 2. Folklore—Japan.]   I. Narahashi, Keiko, ill.   II. Title.   PZ8.U24Mag 1993   398.21—dc20   [E]   92-30132

THE Magic PURSE

retold by Yoshiko Uchida
illustrated by Keiko Narahashi

MARGARET K. McELDERRY BOOKS
New York

Maxwell Macmillan Canada
Toronto

Maxwell Macmillan International
New York Oxford Singapore Sydney

To my parents
—K.N.

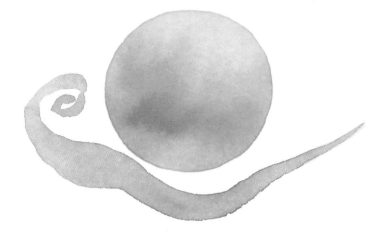

Long ago, in a small mountain village of Japan, there lived a poor young farmer. He scarcely had money for food or clothing, but each month he saved a few coins, hoping to go with his friends to the Iseh shrine in the spring.

But as the months passed, he realized he could never save enough money for the long journey. His friends would have to go without him.

At last, one April morning, when the mist still hung low over the fields of rice, the farmer saw his friends start down the winding dirt road, laughing and singing as they left for the Iseh shrine.

"If only I could go with them," he murmured sadly.

"Go then," a voice deep inside him urged. "Go with them! Hurry!"

Before he quite knew what he was doing, the farmer wrapped some rice cakes in bamboo leaves and hurried down the road after his friends. But no matter how far he walked, he saw no sign of them. Finally he came to a strange road he had never seen before, and believing it to be a shortcut, he hurried on.

Soon dark thunder clouds gathered in the sky, and raging winds and rain tore at his thin straw cape. The farmer realized then that the road had taken him straight to the terrible Black Swamp, filled with murky waters, quicksand, and slithering snakes.

Before he could turn back, a strange young girl came toward him. Her hair hung long and black, and her silvery blue kimono shimmered in the dusky light. Although she walked through the waters of the swamp, she was neither muddy nor wet, and a sad, lonely smile hovered on her lips.

"Don't be afraid," she called in a thin, wavery voice. "I know you are a good kind man, and I have come to ask for your help."

"But…I…I…" the farmer stammered, backing away.

"All I ask," the young girl went on, "is that you take a letter for me to my mother and father who live in the Red Swamp near Osaka."

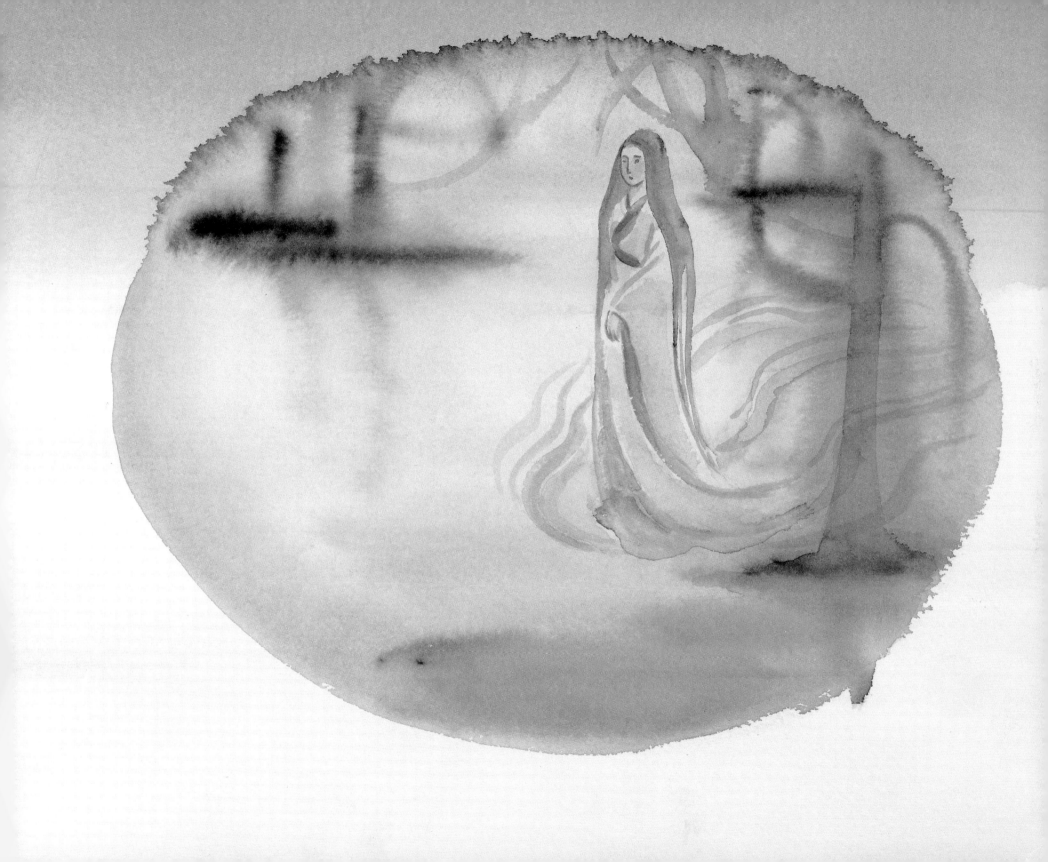

"The Red Swamp!" The farmer gasped. "No one ever comes out of it alive. Besides," he added, "I am on my way to the shrine at Iseh, and I must hurry on."

Tears gathered in the young girl's eyes.

"I am a prisoner of the ruler of this Black Swamp," she sobbed, " and I can never see my parents again. Please, won't you take my letter so they will know I think of them always?"

The gentle farmer could not refuse.

"Ah, that is very sad," he said. "I will do as you ask."

As soon as he had taken the long white envelope she held out, the young girl gave him a small red purse that bulged with gold coins.

"Take this magic purse," she said. "Spend as much as you like, but always leave one coin in it, and the next morning the purse will be full once again."

Then, in a whispery voice that sounded like the flutter of bird wings, she thanked the farmer and disappeared into the swamp as suddenly as she had appeared.

The farmer looked all around but saw only the dark, murky waters of the swamp. From somewhere in the distance, he heard a soft voice calling, ''Don't forget me....Don't forget me....Don't forget...'' Then it died away like an echo in the stillness.

The farmer shivered, yet when he looked up, the clouds were gone and the sun was shining once again.

"I must have dreamed the whole thing," he muttered, but the bulging red coin purse in his hand was very real indeed.

Still wondering about his strange adventure, he set off slowly toward the Red Swamp. As he neared Osaka, he stopped to ask a fish peddler how to get to the swamp.

"The Red Swamp?" the peddler asked, horrified. "You are going to the Red Swamp? Why you will never come out of it alive." And he hurried off, shaking his head.

The farmer next stopped a woodcutter to ask the way, but the
woodcutter shuddered and said, "Only death awaits you there, young
man. I urge you not to go."

By now, the farmer was tempted to throw away the letter, but he
could not forget the beautiful young girl nor her plaintive cry. And so
he trudged on.

At last, he came to the edge of the terrible Red Swamp and saw giant gnarled trees heavy with streamers of moss. Vapors of steam rose from whirlpools, and giant snakes and crocodiles slithered about in the muddy waters.

Soon the farmer was surrounded by darkness. He clapped once to announce his arrival and heard the sound echoing into the silence of the swamp. When he clapped a second time, he saw an old man with a long white beard slowly approaching in a small creaky boat.

"Ah, you have brought word from our daughter," the old man said, as though he had been waiting for the farmer.

"Yes, yes," the farmer said eagerly, handing him the letter. He was anxious to complete his task and be on his way.

But the old man said, "Please, come with me, my friend. And do not be afraid. I know the swamp well and promise no harm will come to you."

The farmer was afraid to go with the old man, and told him he must hurry to the shrine at Iseh to meet his friends. Still the old man stretched out his hand, begging the farmer to come for just a few moments.

Seeing the kindness in the old man's face, the farmer finally stepped into the boat. But the moment he did, he could scarcely keep his eyes open, and he soon fell sound asleep. When he awoke, he found himself in a beautiful golden room. And seated before him were the old man and his wife.

"You have made us so happy," they said. "We can never thank you enough for your kind deed."

Then the old woman brought out one golden lacquer tray after another, each laden with such delicacies as the farmer had never seen before. There were lobsters and sea bream, and fish roe and quail eggs. There were fried bumblebees and turtle chowder and squid and black mushrooms. The farmer ate until he could eat no more.

Then he fell asleep on the thick silken quilts the old woman laid out for him. When he awoke the next morning, he found another golden tray beside his pillow. This one was overflowing with coins of gold.

"They are all for you," the old man and the old woman said, "to thank you for your kind and gentle heart."

The farmer thanked them for their gift and climbed once more into the old man's boat. He blinked for an instant, and immediately found himself again at the edge of the swamp.

"Good-bye, old man," the farmer said, bowing. "I shall never forget you."

When he looked up, the old man had disappeared. Again, it all seemed like a dream, but the gold coins he had received were just as real as his magic purse.

The farmer ran out into the spring sunshine shouting, "I have been in the terrible Red Swamp, and I am alive and well!"

He could now travel to Iseh in a sedan chair, and although he had missed his friends, he thanked the gods at the shrine for his great good fortune.

When he returned to his village, his friends gathered around to hear of his strange adventures in the swamps.

"Only a man with a kind heart would have delivered the letter," they said. "And only a man of courage would have ventured alone into the Red Swamp. Surely you deserve all the riches that have come your way." And they all rejoiced with him.

The farmer now built a new house and bought cows and horses and chickens and pigs. He hired many of the villagers to work for him and always helped anyone in need. But he never ran out of money, for he always left one coin in his purse, and the next morning the purse was full once again.

The farmer thought often of the beautiful young girl in the swamp. And each year when the cherry trees blossomed like white clouds along the riverbank, he took a tray of rice cakes and wine to the Black Swamp and let it float away on the water.

And on the next day, the tray drifted back to him with a tiny flower or
a shiny green leaf on it, and he knew the young girl had received his gift.

She never appeared to the farmer again. But even after many years, he could hear her gentle voice calling, "Don't forget me....Don't forget me...." And for all the remaining days of his life, he never did.